A Whitman TWEEN-AGE Book

In-between books for in-between readers.

TALES FROM

HANS CHRISTIAN ANDERSEN

ABOUT THIS BOOK

Lovely Princess Elise, and her eleven brothers turned into swans . . .

Hans Clodhopper—not wise, not clever—who rode his goat right into the king's palace . . .

The little mermaid who lived in the sea king's palace beneath the sea, but longed to be human . . .

These stories were written more than a hundred years ago. The children of Hans Christian Andersen's Denmark loved them. From Denmark they spread to children all over the world. Now you, too, can meet Hans Clodhopper, and the little mermaid, and many, many more of the Danish storyteller's wonderful friends.

TALES FROM
HANS CHRISTIAN ANDERSEN

as told by
**KATHARINE
CARTER**

illustrated by
**JOSEPH
SMITH**

WHITMAN PUBLISHING COMPANY · Racine, Wisconsin

Library of Congress Catalog Card Number: 65-21123

© Copyright 1965 by Western Publishing Company, Inc.
WHITMAN PUBLISHING COMPANY
RACINE, WISCONSIN
Printed in the U.S.A. by
Western Printing and Lithographing Company

CONTENTS

THE WILD SWANS

Far away, there once lived a king who had eleven sons and one daughter.

The brothers went to school with stars on their breasts and swords at their sides. They wrote with diamond pencils upon slates of gold.

One could tell they were princes because they always knew their lessons perfectly.

Their sister Elise sat on a footstool made of glass. Her picture book cost half a kingdom.

What a happy time she and the princes had!

But, oh, it was not to last, for one day the king married a new—and wicked—queen. The children found out how wicked she was the very first day. At the wedding feast the princes and Elise made believe they had visitors, too.

But the queen would not let them have the cakes and apples they wanted. She put sand in their dishes, saying, "Just make believe it is something good."

And the very next week she sent little Elise to live with some farmers.

Not long after that, the queen made the king believe terrible things about his sons. She talked so much against the princes that the king cared no more for them.

"Fly away and look after yourselves," the wicked queen told the brothers. "Fly about in the shape of birds without voices!"

But she could not do all the harm she wanted. The princes turned into eleven beautiful, white swans. Then they flew away and into a woods.

Early in the morning the swans came to the farmer's house where Elise slept. They circled over the roof, flapping their great wings, but no one heard or saw them. Then they flew away again to a forest near a shore.

One day passed just like another for lonely Elise. Her only toy was a green leaf. She pricked a hole in the leaf and looked through it at the sun. Sometimes when she looked through it she thought she saw her brothers' bright eyes.

At last the day came when Elise was fifteen. She was allowed to return home.

The queen's heart filled with hatred when she saw the beautiful girl. She could not believe anyone could grow up to become as lovely as Elise.

"I wish I could change her into a swan like her brothers," thought the selfish queen. "But I dare not—her father wants to see her."

A few days later the queen took three toads into her marble bath.

To one toad she said, "Sit on Elise's head when she steps into the water. Thus, she will become as dull as you."

To the second she said, "Sit on Elise's forehead. Thus, she may become as ugly as you."

13

And to the third toad she whispered, "Rest upon Elise's heart. Then she will be as evil as you."

As Elise stepped into the water, each toad did as he had been told. But the girl did not seem to notice them. And when she left the marble bath, none of the toads could be seen. But three red poppies were left floating on the water!

Elise was too sweet and kind for witchcraft to have power over her.

The queen was terribly angry. "I will fix you!" she declared. She rubbed walnut juice all over the girl. Then she tangled her long, curly hair.

Poor Elise. No one would have known her. She burst into tears and stole out of the palace.

All day she wandered through the fields, wishing for her brothers. Over and over she thought, "I must find them. I must find them."

By night she had reached a forest. She lay down to sleep on a patch of moss.

All was still and quiet. In the grass around her were hundreds of fireflies flashing their green lights. The whole night long Elise dreamed of her brothers. She dreamed of them reading and playing together

14

as they had done when they were little.

When she awoke the sun was already high. Birds sang happily and the sweet odor of grass filled the air. From nearby came the sound of trickling water.

Elise rushed to it. The water was so clear she could see herself in it. "Oh, I look so ugly!" she thought.

Quickly she dipped her hands into the pond and rubbed her face. Her white skin appeared! "How glad I am, how glad I am!" she cried out.

She washed and washed. Then she plaited her hair. A more beautiful princess could not have been found anywhere!

15

Deeper in the forest, Elise met an old woman carrying a basket.

"Have some of my berries," said the woman.

"Thank you," said Elise and ate them gladly. "I am looking for my brothers. Have you seen eleven princes riding through here?"

"No," the old woman answered. "But yesterday I saw eleven swans swimming in the stream. Each of them wore a golden crown on its head."

She led the princess to the bank of the stream.

"Good-bye, and thank you," Elise said.

She followed the stream until it reached the open shore. There, the whole wide sea spread out before her. Not a boat was in sight.

"How can I go farther?" she wondered.

Just then, she felt a pebble under her foot. She looked at the beach. There were millions of pebbles. There were also pieces of glass and stone washed up by the sea. Each had been made smooth and round by the waves.

Little Elise sighed and picked up a stone. "The sea rolls on and on without stopping," she thought. "I must be just as tireless in my search for my brothers. Thank you, rolling waves, for teaching me your lesson. Someday I believe that you will carry me to my brothers."

Farther along the shore she came upon a wrecked ship. On one of the planks she found white swans' feathers.

"They are so white and clean I shall keep them," Elise decided. She counted eleven and took them with her.

The sun was about to set when something white came flying toward the shore—eleven graceful swans!

Elise hid behind a bush to watch.

The swans had golden crowns on their heads. They floated one behind the other, looking like a long ribbon. Closer and closer they came. Then they plunged down near her, flapping their wings.

The sun sank beneath the water and the swans' feathers disappeared. There stood the eleven princes!

"Oh, oh, it is you!" Elise cried with joy. She sprang into their arms.

The princes shouted with happiness. "Our sister! At last we have found you!"

17

They all were so happy they laughed and cried together.

"We fly as wild swans in the daytime," explained the oldest brother. "But when the sun sets we return to our human shape. That is why we must always find solid ground by evening."

Another brother said, "We do not live here. We fly to a beautiful land across the sea. There is no island on the way where we can pass the night. But there is a small rock in the middle of the ocean."

"It is just large enough for us to rest, huddled together," said another brother. "If it were not for the rock we could never make the journey. It takes two days."

Elise looked at them sadly. "How I wish I could set you free," she said.

"Do not be sad," said the youngest brother. "We are allowed to come home once each year. But we dare stay only eleven days."

The oldest brother took her hand. "We have two more days before we fly across the sea again," he said lovingly. "We can not leave you like this. Have you the courage to come with us?"

"Oh, yes, please take me with you," Elise begged. "But how will you carry me so far?"

"Our wings are strong enough to hold you," the youngest said. "We will make a net to carry you."

They spent the whole night weaving a net of willow and reeds. It was large and strong, and held Elise safely. She lay in it to rest.

When she awoke they were far from land.

"I must be dreaming," she thought. "It is strange to be carried high up over the sea."

She turned, and by her side was a branch with ripe berries on it. She ate the fruit and smiled thankfully up at her youngest brother. His broad wings were shading her.

Higher and higher the swans flew. They sped like arrows through the sky. The first ship Elise saw looked as small as a sea gull.

Near evening, storm clouds gathered in the sky. Elise's heart beat fast with fear.

"Will the sun set before we come to the rock?" she wondered. She looked far ahead, but could not see it. "What shall become of us? It is all my fault," she wept. "If they were not carrying me, my brothers

21

could fly much more swiftly."

The swans seemed to fly faster. But no rock could Elise see. Black clouds rolled overhead. Then lightning streaked the sky.

The sun sank nearly to the edge of the sea. Elise's heart trembled. The swans plunged downward! "No, no!" she cried out.

The swans glided on.

Elise looked at the sun again. It was almost hidden below the water. She turned away. She could not bear to think of what might happen. But after a few seconds she peeped through her fingers. And there ahead was the rock! It seemed no larger than the head of a seal, but it meant safety!

The sun sank. Her feet touched the rock! Her brothers stood around her and Elise was thankful.

"You are so very brave," she told them. "And I am glad you brought me with you."

The thunder rumbled and the waves splashed high, but Elise did not lose her courage again. All night she and the princes stood, soaked by the storm.

Morning brought clear skies. The swans flew on.

24

Long before sunset Elise saw the country they were bound for. Blue mountains reached high into the sky. Palaces stood among forests of cedar.

"How beautiful!" she thought. "If only my brothers could live there with me, not as swans but as princes."

The swans swooped down among the hills. They placed her in front of a large cave over which hung

green vines. Her youngest brother fixed her a bed of leaves and moss. "Now rest and see what you dream of tonight," he said.

"I wish I could dream of a way to set you free," Elise told him. "I can think of nothing else."

Elise covered herself with the leaves and settled down to sleep.

Then, in her dreams, it seemed she was flying up to a cloud-palace. A fairy came out to greet her. The fairy looked just like the woman Elise had met in the forest.

"Your brothers can be freed," the fairy said. "That is, if you have enough courage." She put out her hand in which she held a stinging nettle.

Elise drew back. She wanted to run. But the thought of freeing her brothers kept her from doing it.

"These nettles grow in the cave where you sleep," the fairy said. "They also grow on the graves in the churchyard. You must gather them and crush them with your feet. Their stings will blister your skin, but it is the way to save your brothers.

"When you have crushed the nettles you will

have flax," the fairy went on. "You must spin the flax and knit it into eleven coats. And remember, you are not to speak while you do this. If you speak one word, your brothers will die!" She put the nettle in Elise's hand.

Elise awakened. Her hand burned like fire! It was bright daylight and close by lay a nettle like the one in her dream! She began her task at once.

The princes returned that evening, but Elise did not speak to them.

"Little sister, what is wrong?" they asked, alarmed. "Our stepmother must have cast a spell upon you!"

They looked at Elise's hands and shook their heads sadly. "She is suffering for us," they said.

The youngest brother held her hands in his and wept. And where his tears fell, Elise had no more pain. The burning blisters disappeared.

Elise worked all night long. And all the next day. She was happy to be helping her brothers, and the time flew by. When one coat was finished, she set to work on another at once.

While she was knitting the third coat the sound of horns rang from the mountains. The sound came

A Whitman TWEEN-AGE Book

In-between books for in-between readers.

nearer, and the sound of dogs barking fiercely.

Elise trembled with fear. "What is happening?" she said to herself, while she gathered the nettles. Quickly she dashed into the cave with the bundle.

Moments later, huntsmen stood at the cave opening. The most handsome of them stepped forward. "Why are you here, beautiful maiden?" he asked.

Elise shook her head. She hid her hands under her apron.

The man bowed and said, "I am the king. You must not remain here. If you are as kind as you are beautiful, you shall live in my palace." He lifted her up on his horse.

Tears rolled down Elise's cheeks. She wrung her hands with worry.

"I only want to make you happy," the king told her. He held her in front of him on the horse and galloped off.

The king's palace was wondrous! In the halls great fountains sparkled in the sunlight. Every room was filled with fine furniture and velvet curtains.

But none of it interested Elise. Nor did the silk gowns and the jewels she was given. "My brothers!

How can I help them now?" was her every thought.

When the king saw how beautiful Elise was in the new clothes, he bowed very low. "I want to take you for my bride," he said, and kissed her hand.

Poor Elise could not say a word. Neither did a smile come to her lips or eyes.

The king ordered musicians to play at the wedding. Then there was a rich feast and dancing. But Elise's heart ached.

"If only I could finish the coats," she wished again and again.

After the celebration the king led her to a small room. On the floor was a costly green carpet. Hangings on the walls made it look like a cave.

"He has had it made to look like the place where he found me!" Elise thought in surprise.

She turned and saw her bundle of flax in a corner. And from the ceiling hung the coats she had finished!

"Now you may dream you are back in your old home," the king said tenderly. "And you can go on with your knitting, if you wish."

Elise's heart beat fast with happiness. Her eyes

filled with love for the king. She smiled at him and kissed his hand.

And as the days passed she loved him more dearly. Every hour she thought, "If only I could tell him of my brothers!" But not one word could she speak. Silently she continued her task.

As she began the seventh coat, Elise saw there was not enough flax to finish it.

"How will I get to the churchyard and gather more nettles?" she wondered. "But I must take the chance. I can not give up now."

That night, she bravely crept out of the palace. Through the empty streets she hurried. At last she came to the churchyard.

But, oh, what an ugly sight was before her! Around a gravestone sat a group of long-haired, wrinkled witches!

Elise had to pass close by them. She could feel their evil eyes staring at her. Bravely she gathered the nettles. Then she hurried back to the palace.

Some days later, Elise noticed that the handsome king looked pale. He seemed sad. It troubled her. Her eyes filled with tears as she thought, "My poor brothers! And now the good, kind king."

Meanwhile, she finished the tenth coat. "Only one more to make," she sighed with relief.

Then she saw there was not a single nettle left!

Once again Elise went to the churchyard. The king followed, but she did not see him.

The king knew that Elise left her room at night. He had also heard tales the witches had spread about. They had told everyone they met that Elise was one of them.

"It is not true," the king had replied whenever he heard the tale. But again and again he heard it, and it made him very sad. So that was why he followed Elise, to see for himself.

Elise opened the iron gates. There around a gravestone were the hateful witches!

The good king waited outside, but he saw the witches, too. Brokenhearted, he turned away. "My people must judge her," he said with sorrow.

And the people of his kingdom said Elise must die.

From her pleasant room, Elise was taken to an underground prison. It was dark and damp. The wind whistled through the barred windows.

She shivered but somehow kept up her hopes. For they had given her the nettles she had gathered and the coats she had knit. "Use these for covering instead of silk and velvet!" the angry people had said.

"They do not know it is what I want most!" Elise thought happily, and began work again.

Near evening she heard wings flapping near the window. It was her youngest brother! She jumped up and wept with joy. This night could well be her last, but her brothers had come! And the eleventh

coat was now almost finished.

Quickly, Elise went back to work. And even the little mice in the prison tried to help her! They ran back and forth, dragging the nettles to her. A bird sat in the window and sang sweetly all night long.

At dawn the eleven princes stood at the palace gate. "We want to see the king," they told the guard.

"He is still asleep," the guard answered.

The brothers begged and begged.

There was such a clatter, the king awakened. He came to the gate and asked, "What goes on? Who are you and what do you wish?"

At that moment, sunlight streamed from the heavens. The princes disappeared. But eleven wild swans flew overhead.

Soon the townspeople came rushing to the palace. "We have come to see the witch die!" they cried.

Good, beautiful Elise was brought to the courtyard in a cart pulled by a lame horse. And even now she did not stop knitting on the eleventh coat. The other ten lay at her feet.

The crowd rushed toward her, shouting, "She is a witch!" They reached out to take hold of her.

Elise trembled with fright, but kept on working.

As they reached for her again, eleven swans swooped down! They perched on the cart, flapping their wings!

The people stepped back in silence.

Elise snatched up the coats and threw them over the swans.

Eleven handsome princes stood up. But the youngest had a wing in place of one arm. Elise had not been able to finish the second sleeve.

"Now I dare speak," she said firmly. "I am innocent. I am not a witch."

The crowd stared in wonder. "It is a sign from heaven," they whispered. "She is innocent."

They hung their heads with shame.

Poor Elise was so weary she fell over in her brothers' arms.

The king picked a beautiful white flower from a bush. He placed it in Elise's hand. She awoke and smiled joyfully.

All the church bells began to ring. The birds sang. And the king and Elise strolled, arm in arm, into the palace.

THE NIGHTINGALE

Once, long long ago, a strange and wonderful thing happened to a certain emperor of China. Because it was so wonderful, the story must be told again, lest it be forgotten.

The emperor's palace was the most beautiful that can be imagined. It was made entirely of the finest porcelain.

Outside, there was a garden. In the garden grew unusual flowers. The most beautiful ones had little silver bells tied to them. Their merry tinkle made everyone stop and listen. This garden was so large that even the gardener did not know where it ended.

If one walked on and on through the garden, one came to a woods with deep lakes. The woods reached out to the sea where ships sailed right under the branches of the trees. In these trees lived a nightingale which sang very, very beautifully.

Every night a poor fisherman, who had much to do, heard the nightingale's song. He always stopped to enjoy the lovely sound.

"Heavens, how beautifully it sings," he always said.

Then he had to attend to his work and forgot about the bird.

But each night he heard it again and exclaimed, "Heavens, how beautiful it is!"

Travelers from every country came to see the emperor. They admired everything, and most of all the palace and the gardens.

But when they heard the nightingale they said,

"This is better than anything."

Back home, they told everyone about the bird.

Many men wrote books about the town, the palace, and the gardens. And each of them said, "The nightingale is the most wonderful of all."

These books went around the world. Some of them reached the emperor.

He sat in his chair reading them and smiling.

"How nice to have such things said of my palace and gardens," he thought. Then he sat up straight as he read, "But the nightingale is better than anything there."

"What is this?" the emperor wondered. "The nightingale? Why have I never heard of it? Is there such a bird in my kingdom?"

He called to his gentleman-in-waiting, "Come here at once."

The man entered and bowed.

"This book says there is a wonderful bird called a nightingale here," said the emperor. "It is said to be greater than anything in my great kingdom! Why have I not been told about it?"

The gentleman-in-waiting bowed again. "I have

never heard of such a bird, your Majesty," he said. "It has never been presented at court."

"I wish it here this very evening to sing for me," the emperor commanded. "Imagine the world knowing about it and not I!"

"I will seek it and I will find it, your Majesty," said the gentleman-in-waiting.

He bowed and backed away.

"But where is this bird to be found?" he wondered.

He went upstairs and downstairs. He looked in every room. No one he met had heard of the bird.

He returned to the emperor and said, "It must be a myth, your Majesty. Books are often writers' inventions."

"But this one was sent to me by the Emperor of Japan!" cried the emperor. "It must be true. I say that the nightingale must sing here tonight. If it does not appear I shall have the whole court trampled upon."

"Tsing-pe!" said the gentleman-in-waiting, and away he ran.

He raced up and down the stairs.

44

He went into all the rooms again.

Half the court ran with him, for none of them wished to be trampled upon. They asked the servants, "Have you heard of the nightingale?"

At last a kitchen maid said, "The nightingale? I know it very well. Each evening I am allowed to take food to my sick mother. She lives by the shore, and sometimes I am tired and rest in the woods. That is when I hear the bird. It sings so gloriously it brings tears to my eyes."

"Little kitchen maid," the gentleman-in-waiting said excitedly, "please help me find the bird. I will see to it that you keep your job forever."

"Certainly. Come with me," she replied, and led the way to the woods.

Half the court followed.

As they hurried along, a cow bellowed.

"Oh," whispered a young courtier, "there it is. What a strong voice for so little a creature."

"No, no, that is a cow bellowing," the maid explained. "We are a long way from the place."

Then frogs began to croak.

"How beautiful!" declared another courtier. "It is like the tinkling of church bells."

The maid shook her head. "No, no. Those are frogs. But we will soon come to the right place."

They hurried on, and shortly they heard a bird singing.

"Listen, there it is!" the maid said happily.

She pointed to a tiny gray bird up among the branches.

The gentleman-in-waiting stared in amazement. "Is that it? How unimportant it looks!" he cried.

"Seeing so many people must have frightened its colors away."

"Little nightingale," the kitchen maid called. "Our gracious emperor wishes you to sing for him."

"With the greatest of pleasure," said the nightingale.

It warbled again in a most delightful way.

"It sings like crystal bells!" declared the gentleman-in-waiting. "See the movement in its little throat! It is odd we have never heard of it before. I am sure it will be well thought of at court."

The nightingale asked, "Shall I sing for the emperor again?" It thought his majesty was present.

"Dear little bird, not here," said the gentleman-in-waiting. "I have the honor to command your presence at court tonight. The emperor will be very pleased with your singing."

"But my song sounds best among the trees," the bird told him. However, it went back to the palace with them.

The servants had been busy.

The walls and floors, which were china, shone by the light of thousands of lamps.

Beautiful, tinkling flowers were in every room. A soft breeze floated through the whole palace. It was what made the bells ring.

The emperor sat in a large room. Near him had been placed a gold rod on which the nightingale was to perch.

The entire court was there, waiting to hear the wonderful song of the bird.

Even the little kitchen maid was peeping from behind a door. "And now I am a cook!" she said to herself proudly.

The bird sang beautifully. It did its very best.

As the emperor listened, tears ran down his cheeks.

"You shall have my gold slipper to wear around your neck," he told the bird.

"Thank you, your gracious Majesty," the nightingale replied. "Your tears are my reward. The tears of an emperor have wonderful power."

And then it burst into its sweet song again.

The ladies of the court stared in surprise. "The bird is the most delightful charmer we have ever seen," they said. They took some water in their mouths and tried to make the same beautiful sound.

Even the chambermaids agreed that the little bird's song was too marvelous to believe. And that is saying a lot, as they are usually hard to please.

"Dear little nightingale, you shall live here always," the emperor announced. "You shall have your own cage. You shall be taken for a walk every day. I shall place twelve footmen at your service."

And twelve footmen the nightingale was given! When it went outdoors, each footman held a ribbon which was tied around its legs.

The townspeople looked at it in wonder.

Often when two people met, one said "Night," and the other answered "Gale."

Some named their children after the bird. But not one of them could sing.

One day a large package came for the emperor.

"Another book about our bird," he said happily as he opened the package.

But inside was not another book about the nightingale. Instead, there was an artificial bird.

"How beautiful!" shouted the emperor, holding it in his hand. "It is made to look exactly like my nightingale! And it is covered with diamonds and rubies!"

He wound up the little artificial bird and it began to sing. Its song was very like that of the real bird! It even shook its gold and silver tail!

Then the emperor looked at the writing on a ribbon around the bird's neck. He read, "The Emperor of Japan's nightingale is poor compared to the Emperor of China's."

"How beautiful! Now they must sing together," cried all the court.

The real nightingale and the artificial one did sing together. But they did not do very well. The real bird sang in its own way and the artificial bird

sang only one of the newest waltzes.

"I find no fault with it," said the music master. "It is in time and correct in every way."

So then the artificial bird had to sing alone. Everyone liked it. Because of its jewels it was also prettier to look at. And after it had sung its tune three and thirty times, it was not tired.

The court begged, "Please, let us hear it again."

"No, it is the real bird's turn now," said the

emperor. He turned and looked around the room. "Where is it? What is the meaning of this?"

The real nightingale was not to be found.

"How terrible!" the emperor said sadly. "It must have gone back to its own green woods."

"Well, we have the best one," the court said.

They wound the artificial bird and listened to its tune the thirty-fourth time.

"This is far better than the real nightingale," the music master said. "We know what this one will

sing every time. But with the other bird we never knew."

The next Sunday the music master showed the artificial bird at church.

"It is wonderful!" the people agreed when they heard it sing.

That is, all but one agreed. The fisherman who had heard the real nightingale shook his head.

"It is nice," he said, "and almost like the real bird. But there is something wanting."

When the artificial bird was returned to the palace the emperor placed it near his bed.

56

"This little bird must have a title," he said thoughtfully. "It shall be called Chief Imperial Singer-of-the-Bedchamber."

The music master wrote twenty-five books about the artificial bird. And everyone in the country said they read the books. If they had not, they would have been thought stupid.

Things went on this way for a whole year. The emperor and all his people knew the artificial bird's song by heart. They sang it happily every day.

But one evening when it was singing, something happened.

Whizz, whirr, it went. The song stopped!

The emperor jumped out of bed.

"Get my doctor!" he yelled to a servant.

Of course the doctor could do nothing for the bird.

He said, "Send for the watchmaker."

"This little bird is almost worn out," the watchmaker told them. "But I will try to fix the works so it can run a little."

The emperor and all his court were greatly troubled.

57

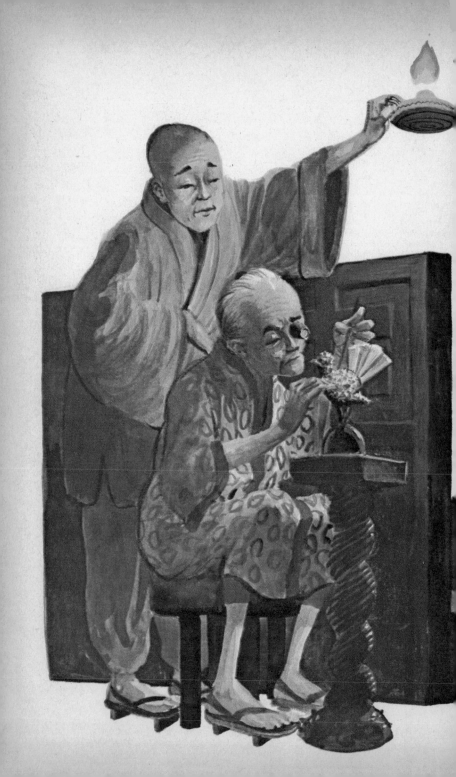

Heavyhearted, the emperor said, "Now I shall dare have it sing only once a year."

Five years passed, and then sadness came upon the whole country.

The emperor was taken ill. It was thought he could not live.

He lay in his bed under an open window. The moonlight streamed in upon him and the artificial bird beside him.

The emperor felt as if there were a weight on his chest. He could scarcely breathe. His mind began to wander and he imagined many things.

"Death is sitting on my chest," he thought. "It is wearing a golden crown and holding my sword in its hands."

Among the folds in the curtains he saw many faces. "They are my good and bad deeds," he said. "They are asking, 'Do you remember?'"

Beads of sweat stood on his forehead. "Music, music!" he cried. "Precious little golden bird, sing, sing!"

The bird stood silent. There was no one to wind it.

And then, suddenly, there came through the window a lovely song! It was the living nightingale perched in a tree outside.

As it sang, the emperor's thoughts cleared. The paleness left his cheeks and his body became a little stronger.

The nightingale kept on singing.

"Thank you, thank you," the emperor murmured. "How can I ever repay you?"

"You rewarded me long ago," the nightingale told him. "Tears came to your eyes the first time I

sang for you, and I shall never forget it. Those are the jewels that make me happy. But sleep now, and wake up strong."

The nightingale sang again, and the emperor slept.

The sun shone brightly when he awoke next morning. And the little bird was beside him singing gaily.

"Stay with me always," the emperor begged. "You need sing only when you like. I shall break the artificial bird into a thousand pieces."

"Do not do that," said the nightingale. "It did all it could, so keep it just as it is. I can not build my nest in the palace, but I will come to your window often. I will sing to make you happy, and thoughtful, too. But you must promise one thing."

"Anything!" the emperor declared. He got up and put on his robes.

"Just one thing I ask," said the nightingale. "Tell no one you have a bird that tells you everything."

Then it flew away.

The court attendants came quietly into the room. They feared their beloved emperor was dead.

But there he stood, saying, "Good morning!"

THUMBELINA

There was once a woman who longed for a very tiny child, but she had no idea where to find one.

At last she went to an old witch. "I am most eager for a very, very little child," she said. "Will you please help me to find one?"

"Indeed, yes. That will be easy," said the witch.

She gave the woman a grain of barleycorn. "It is not like the kind that grows in the farmers' fields," she said. "Plant it in a flowerpot. You will see what you will see."

The woman gave the witch twelve coins and thanked her. Then she hurried home and planted the seed.

Right away green leaves began to appear. Next, a tall stem. And last, a beautiful blossom with its petals tightly closed.

"Oh, how lovely!" said the woman, and kissed the flower. As she did so, the red and gold petals opened.

"A beautiful tulip!" the woman said happily.

She looked inside the tulip and could scarcely believe her eyes. For curled up there was a very tiny little girl!

"My wish is granted!" cried the woman, as she looked at the tiny child. "You are only half as large as my thumb. I shall call you Thumbelina."

A polished walnut shell became a bed for Thumbelina. Violet petals made a soft mattress. At night the woman covered her with a rose leaf.

During the daytime Thumbelina played on a table where there was a bowl of flowers. She used a tulip petal for a boat. Two horsehairs were her oars. As she floated around in the bowl she sang

sweetly with a tiny silvery voice.

One night while Thumbelina was asleep, a horrid toad hopped through the open window and right onto the table beside her.

"What a beautiful wife for my son!" said the toad. She picked up the walnut shell with Thumbelina in it. Then she hopped out the window into the garden. There, the toad and her son lived beside a brook.

The son looked just like his mother. "Cr-roak, crr-roak," was all he could say when he saw the lovely little girl.

"Don't speak so loud or you will wake her," the old toad said to her son. "She might try to run away.

"We will place her on one of the water-lily leaves in the brook so she can not escape. Then we will sweep out the stateroom under the marsh. You can keep house there together."

The old toad took Thumbelina and the bed to a leaf in the middle of the brook. She left the tiny girl there and hurried back to the marsh.

Quickly she set to work making the room ready

for her new daughter-in-law.

Poor little Thumbelina woke up early next morning. When she saw water all about she was frightened. She hopped out of the walnut shell and stood on the leaf.

"What shall I do? What shall I do?" she asked herself and began to weep.

Before long the toad and her son came to the leaf where Thumbelina was standing.

"Here is my son," the mother toad said to her. "He will be your husband and you will live happily together."

"Cr-roak, crr-roak, crrr-roak," was all the son could say for himself.

Then the mother toad and her son took the little bed and swam off with it.

Thumbelina sat down on the leaf and wept and wept. She knew they were taking her bed to their mud house and they would be back for her.

She did not want to marry the toad.

She did not want to live with the horrid mother toad.

It was all too terrible to be true.

All the time the little fishes in the water had been listening to what was said. At last they leaped out of the water to look at the little maiden.

When they saw how sweet and tiny she was, they felt sorry for her.

"She must never go to live with those toads!" they said. "We will help her."

The fishes swam to the leaf where Thumbelina sat. They bit through the stem that held the leaf and she floated away.

The water sparkled in the sunshine. The trees waved their branches as if to welcome her. And the birds sang, "What a charming little maiden!"

Thumbelina was happy.

After she had sailed far away from the two toads, a great cockchafer flew down to her. He grabbed her with his claws and carried her up into a tree.

Little Thumbelina trembled with fright. "What is going to happen to me now?" she wondered.

The cockchafer brought her honey from the flowers to eat. "You are very, very pretty," he told her.

Before long, all the other cockchafers in the tree came to visit Thumbelina. They stared and stared

70

at her, which made her most uncomfortable.

One of them said, "How strange she is! She has only two legs! And no feelers! How sad."

"Shameful, shameful!" said a lady cockchafer. "She looks like a real person! Did you ever see anything so ugly?"

Thumbelina was heartbroken. It was terrible to be so ugly that even the cockchafers would have nothing to do with her.

All summer Thumbelina lived alone in the forest.

She wove a bed with blades of grass and hung it under a big leaf. Thus, the rain did not fall upon her.

She ate the honey from the flowers and drank the dew that formed at night.

When winter came the trees and flowers faded and died. Even the big leaf that covered Thumbelina's bed fell to the ground. Her clothes were torn.

And then it began to snow. Thumbelina shivered. She put a dry leaf around her and crept through the forest hunting food.

There was a grain field close by. But the grain

had been cut and nothing was left but roots.

Thumbelina trembled with the cold and wandered on.

At last she came to the home of a field mouse under a root. She stood before the door like a little beggar girl and asked for a bit of barleycorn.

"You poor little thing," said the field mouse. "Come right in and have something to eat."

Inside, the tiny girl was almost overcome by the warm, pleasant house. There was a whole room filled with corn. And a cozy kitchen with food in it, too.

The kind field mouse said, "You may stay the winter with me, if you like. But you must keep my house clean and tell me stories. I enjoy hearing stories."

Thumbelina thought she must be dreaming. "I will do it gladly," she said.

One day the field mouse said, "My neighbor will be coming to visit. He wears fine clothes and has a big home. You would do well to take him for a husband."

The visitor arrived. He wore a black velvet

73

coat. Little Thumbelina sighed. He was a mole.

"Please sing for my neighbor," the field mouse said to her.

"Cockchafer, cockchafer, fly away home," Thumbelina sang softly.

The mole smiled at her lovingly. He seemed to like her sweet voice. But he said nothing. He was very prim and proper.

After a while he spoke up. "My home is in the ground and has many large rooms. I never go out in the sunshine. I can't bear it or the flowers and trees. Truly, I have never seen them."

Thumbelina was troubled. Imagine anyone not liking the beautiful world outside! She could never marry such an odd person.

"I have dug a passage from my house to this one," the mole went on. "Please honor me with a visit."

Thumbelina and the field mouse followed the mole through the tunnel. He carried a piece of touchwood in his mouth. The wood glowed like fire and lighted the way.

In the middle of the passage they came upon a

dead swallow. Thumbelina was sorry to see that the little bird had frozen to death. She knew how it felt to be terribly cold.

The mole pushed the bird aside and said, "He won't 'tweet-tweet' any more. And of what use is his 'tweet-tweet'? He has to starve or freeze in winter."

That night Thumbelina could not sleep, for she kept thinking of the swallow.

"It may be the one who sang to me in the summer," she thought. She got up and wove a blanket of hay. Then she carried it out to the bird.

"Farewell, little swallow," Thumbelina said. "And thank you for your sweet songs."

As she put the blanket around him, she held him against her heart. The bird moved a tiny bit! He was only half frozen.

Thumbelina was happy to know that her warm hands and the blanket had saved him.

"Thank you very much, little maiden," said the swallow. "I will soon be quite strong and able to fly again."

"Oh, no. It is snowing outside," she said. "Stay in your warm bed. I will take care of you."

She hurried away and returned with water in a flower petal for him to drink.

The rest of the winter Thumbelina took care of the swallow. But she did not tell the field mouse and the mole. Why they did not like him she would never understand.

When spring came the bird was strong and ready to fly.

"Come with me far away into the green wood," he said to Thumbelina. "I will carry you upon my back."

"I fear I can not," she told him. "It would not be nice for me to leave the field mouse that way. She has been very kind to me."

"Farewell, little maiden. Thank you for your care," sang the swallow. And out of the passage and into the bright sunshine he flew.

Thumbelina's eyes filled with tears. She would miss the swallow very much.

"And I wish I could be out in the green world," she said to herself. The new corn had grown high

77

over the home of the field mouse. It was like a forest to the tiny girl who was only an inch tall.

Some weeks later the field mouse said, "You are to be married, Thumbelina. The mole has asked for your hand. It is good fortune for you, poor little maid. We must make some pretty wedding clothes for you."

Thumbelina was kept busy weaving the cloth. The kind field mouse also hired four spiders to weave day and night.

Every evening the mole came to visit. "We will be married when summer is over," he told Thumbelina.

She blinked her eyes, trying to keep back her tears. She did not like the tiresome mole.

As often as she could, Thumbelina went outdoors and tried to see the blue sky above the tall corn. And each time she wished to see the swallow again.

Autumn came and Thumbelina's clothes were ready.

"In four weeks your wedding will take place," the field mouse told her.

Thumbelina wept bitterly and said, "I will not marry the hateful mole!"

"Nonsense," said the field mouse. "Do not be contrary, or I will have to bite you with my sharp teeth."

The little maiden's heart was broken. To live under the earth would be dreadful!

She went to the door and looked up at the sky once more. "Farewell, bright sunshine!" she cried, stretching her arms upward.

Then she walked into the field where the corn had been cut. She found a little red flower still blooming there.

"Farewell, farewell," Thumbelina said, putting her hands around it. "Please speak to the swallow for me, if you see him."

"Tweet, tweet," a bird sang overhead.

Thumbelina looked up. It was the swallow flying by!

"Oh, I am happy to see you!" she said to the bird.

She told him about the ugly mole she was supposed to marry and how she would hate to live under the ground. Tears ran down her cheeks as she talked.

"I am on my way to the warm countries," said the swallow. "Please come with me, Thumbelina. You saved my life. Now let me help you."

"Yes, yes, I will come with you," Thumbelina said gladly.

She seated herself on the bird's back and tied her sash to one of his strongest feathers.

The swallow flew high over the forests and seas. And then over snow-covered mountains.

At last they came to the warm countries. The sun shone brightly on vines heavy with blue and purple grapes. There were trees filled with oranges and lemons. The air was sweet with blossoms.

But the swallow flew still farther. The countries became more and more beautiful.

Under a huge tree by a lake, Thumbelina saw a marble palace. At the top were many swallows' nests.

"That is my home," said the swallow. "But it is not right for you to live there. You may choose one of the lovely flowers and I will put you on it."

"That will be wonderful!" Thumbelina said. She clapped her tiny hands with joy, and chose a beautiful white flower. The swallow flew down to it.

But what a surprise awaited Thumbelina. In the center of the flower stood a tiny little man! He had a crown on his head and wings on his shoulders. He was the king of the flowers and was just a little taller than Thumbelina.

"How beautiful he is!" Thumbelina whispered to the swallow.

The king bowed and said "You are the most charming maiden I have ever seen." He took off

his crown and put it on her head. "What is your name, and will you please be my wife?"

"Yes," Thumbelina answered softly.

Just then, out of every flower there came a tiny little man or woman. They were lords and ladies, and each had a gift for Thumbelina. The most perfect gift was a pair of shining white wings that had belonged to a great fly.

The king fastened them to her back and said, "I am the King of the Flowers and you are the Queen. Now, you can fly with me to every flower."

There was great joy as the swallow sang the wedding song.

"You are too charming to be called Thumbelina," said the flower elf. "We shall call you Maia."

Only the little swallow was sad, for he hated to part from her.

"Good-bye, good-bye," he called as he flew far, far away to Denmark.

There he found a cozy place above the window of the man who tells fairy tales. To him he sang, "Tweet-tweet! Tweet-tweet!"

And that is how we got this story.

HANS CLODHOPPER
(or NUMBSKULL JACK)

Once upon a time there was a huge palace far out in the country. In it lived an old gentleman and his two clever sons.

The sons made up their minds to ask for the king's daughter in marriage. For the king's messengers had told everyone in the kingdom that she would choose anyone who could speak well for himself. The sons thought that they had a very good chance.

84

They had only one week to prepare for their visit to the palace. But that was all they needed, as they both knew many things.

"I know all the words in the dictionary! I can also repeat by heart everything in the newspaper," said one.

The second son replied, "I know all the laws of the town. I can talk about state affairs. And I can do very fine embroidery!"

"I shall win the king's daughter!" they both declared, very sure of themselves.

The son who could repeat the dictionary and newspaper had a black horse. And the one who was learned in government had a milk-white horse. Just as they were about to mount their horses, a third brother joined them.

Yes, there were three sons. Only no one ever paid any attention to the third one. He was not wise and clever, so they called him Hans Clodhopper.

"Where are you going in your best clothes?" Hans Clodhopper asked them.

"To the royal court, to talk the princess into marrying one of us," they said. "Haven't you heard the news? Everyone is talking about it."

And then they told him what the king's messengers had said.

"Save us all! Then I must go, too!" said Hans Clodhopper.

His brothers just laughed and rode away.

Hans Clodhopper hurried to his father. "Give me a horse, please," he begged. "I want to get married, too. If the princess takes me she takes me, and if she doesn't I shall take her anyway."

"Nonsense, I shall give you no horse," the father answered with a shrug. "Why, you have nothing you can say for yourself! Your brothers are smart lads."

"If I may not have a horse, I will take the billy goat," said Hans Clodhopper. "The billy goat is mine and he can carry me very well."

And so he seated himself on the goat and off they galloped. And what a pace they went!

The clever brothers rode along in silence. They were too busy thinking to talk. Each was storing up ideas for his speech to the princess.

When Hans Clodhopper caught up with them he

shouted "Hello! Here I come! See what I found on the road!" He showed them a dead crow.

"What in the world will you do with that?" they asked.

"I shall give it to the king's daughter," said Hans.

The brothers laughed loudly and said, "What a fine gift!" Then they galloped on ahead of their brother.

Farther along, Hans Clodhopper rode up beside them again.

"Hello, here I come!" he called. "See, one doesn't find such as this every day!" He held up an old wooden shoe.

"Clodhopper," said the brothers, "is the princess to have that, too?"

"Indeed, she is!" said Hans.

The brothers rode on again, bursting with laughter.

And then Hans Clodhopper caught up with them a third time.

"What have you got now?" the brothers snickered.

Hans Clodhopper exclaimed, "Won't the princess

be happy at receiving this!"

He showed them his pockets filled with sand.

"Mercy upon us!" cried the brothers. "It is only sand from the ditch!"

"That it is," said Hans Clodhopper, "and the finest there is! You can hardly hold it."

The two clever brothers rode swiftly. They reached the town gates an hour before Hans.

There was great excitement. A hundred men stood in lines six deep. They were given tickets in order of their arrival. Each one seemed to wish he were ahead of the others.

The people of the town were crowded at the palace windows. "We want to see the princess receive these suitors!" they called to one another.

Alas, as each suitor went before the princess he lost his voice!

"No good!" said the princess. "Away with him!"

Now came the brother who could repeat the dictionary. But believe it or not, he had forgotten

everything while standing in line!

The floor creaked under him. He looked up at the mirror on the ceiling. "How silly!" he thought, as he saw himself upside down.

It was terrible! And the stove was red with heat. He wiped his brow and exclaimed, "It is so hot in here!"

"That is because my father is roasting cockerels today," the princess said.

He had not expected her to talk of such plain things. He felt like a fool. Not one clever thing could he think of to say.

"No good!" said the king's daughter. "Away with him!"

Then came the second brother.

"There is a fearful heat in here," said he.

"Yes, we are roasting cockerels today," the princess told him.

"What did—what?" he stammered.

"Never! Away with him!" said the princess.

And then it was Hans Clodhopper's turn. He rode the billy goat right into the room!

"What a hot fire you have there," he said to the king's daughter.

"We are roasting cockerels," she replied.

"That is just right," said Hans Clodhopper. "Perhaps I can get a crow roasted, too."

"Why, yes," said the princess. "Do you have something to put it in? I have neither pot nor pan."

"Oh, yes," Hans Clodhopper said happily. He brought out the wooden shoe and put the great, black crow in it.

"You have enough for a whole meal," the princess said, smiling pleasantly. "But where will we get some dripping to pour over it?"

"Right here!" Hans Clodhopper declared. He took a handful of sand out of his pocket.

"Now, I like that," said the princess. "You have an answer for everything. You have something to say for yourself. I will have you for my husband. But do you know that all we have said will be in the paper tomorrow? There in the window sit the alderman and clerks. The alderman is the worst. He never gets anything right."

"The alderman is a high officer of the town," said Hans Clodhopper. "I must give him the best thing I have." He emptied his pockets and threw the sand at the man.

"That was a smart thing to do," the princess said with delight. "I shall try to be as clever as you."

And so Hans Clodhopper became king. He gained a wife and sat upon a throne.

We have this straight from the alderman's newspaper, but it is not to be depended upon.

THE EMPEROR'S NEW CLOTHES

Long ago there lived an emperor who liked new clothes so much that he spent all his money on them. He had a different costume for every hour in the day.

The emperor cared nothing about his soldiers. Neither did he care about the theater nor about driving in the woods. The one important thing to him was showing off his many fine suits.

94

People usually say of their king, "He is in his council chamber." But of the emperor they said, "He is in his wardrobe."

Life was very gay in the great town where the emperor lived. Many visitors came there every day. But one day among the visitors were two cheats.

"We are weavers. We make the finest cloth ever seen," they told everyone. "Our colors are more beautiful than other weavers'. And our cloth has a very special quality. It becomes invisible to anyone who is unfit for his work," they said. "Neither can

it be seen by those who are stupid."

"Clothes made of this cloth would be marvelous to have!" thought the emperor. "By wearing them I could discover which men in my empire are not fit for the offices they hold. I would know which are wise and which are fools!"

The emperor smiled to himself and handed the cheats a wad of money. "Begin at once to weave the cloth for me," he told them.

The cheats hurried away and put up two looms. They pretended to be weaving, but they had nothing at all on the looms.

The very next day they went to the emperor and said, "We need more money. We must have fine silk and gold thread."

The emperor gave them the money.

The cheats put all of it in their own pockets and sat by their empty looms.

As time passed the emperor wished to know how much cloth was ready. But he felt a little uncomfortable about going to see it. He remembered that a stupid person could not see the cloth. Neither could one who was unfit for his post.

"Of course, I have no reason to be afraid to go," the emperor told himself. "However, I would rather send someone else first."

Everyone in the town had heard about the strange power of the cloth. It made all of them want to find out how stupid their neighbors were.

"I will send my faithful old minister of state," the emperor finally decided. "He will see how the cloth looks, for he is a clever man. And no one does his duty better than he."

So the good minister went to the room where the cheats were. He found them working busily at the empty looms.

"Heaven help me!" thought the old man. He opened his eyes wide. "Goodness, I don't see one thing!" But he dared not say so.

"Step closer," said one of the cheats. "Is it not a beautiful color and pattern?"

"Mercy, am I so stupid?" thought the minister. "Am I not fit for my post? It will never do for me to say I can not see the cloth."

"Well, sir, don't you have anything to say?" asked the other cheat.

"Oh, it is lovely, very lovely," the old minister said. "A gay pattern and beautiful colors. I will tell the emperor I am greatly pleased with it."

"We are glad of that," said the cheats. They named the colors and talked about the pattern.

The minister listened so he could report to the emperor.

Soon after that, the cheats asked for more money. And silk and gold, too. They said they needed it to go on with their weaving.

A few more days passed and the emperor sent another honest statesman to see the cloth.

The same thing happened. The honest statesman looked and looked and looked. He saw nothing but empty looms.

"Is not this a pretty piece of cloth?" asked one of the cheats.

"I am no fool," thought the statesman. "It must be that I am not fit for my office. But that is strange. However, I shall not let on."

The second cheat talked about the colors and pattern.

"It is very wonderful," the statesman agreed.

100

Back at the palace he told the emperor, "The cloth is enchanting, your Majesty."

By now all the people in the town were excited about the splendid cloth.

The emperor was more eager than ever to see it while it was still on the looms.

"Come with me," he ordered several of his officers. He also ordered the minister and the statesman to follow them to the weavers' room.

They found the cheats still pretending they were busy. Their looms were as empty as ever.

"The cloth is splendid!" cried both the minister and the statesman. "See, your Majesty, what marvelous design! What colors!"

They pointed to the empty looms, feeling sure the others could see the cloth.

"Gracious me!" thought the emperor. "I can not see one thing! Am I stupid? Am I not fit to be emperor? Nothing could be more terrible for me than that!"

He stared again in disbelief. Then aloud, he said, "It is beautiful! I like it very much."

No matter what, the emperor would not think

of admitting he saw nothing at all.

The other officers exclaimed, "It is truly wonderful, your Majesty! You must wear a suit made of it in the parade next week."

There was great rejoicing among them. So much so, that the emperor said to the cheats, "You shall become the Imperial Court Weavers!"

The cheats sat up the whole night before the parade. They lighted sixteen candles, so that people could see how busy they were.

They pretended to take the cloth off the looms.

They pretended to be cutting out the suit with huge scissors.

And they made believe they were sewing away with needles that had no thread in them.

At dawn they said, "Now the emperor's new clothes are ready."

The emperor himself went to get his fine new suit. With him were the men who had been to the weavers' room before.

The cheats lifted their arms as if they were holding up something.

"See, here are the trousers! Here is the coat!

And here is your fine cape!" said one.

The other cheat added, "It is as light as a spider's web. One would think one had nothing on, but that is the beauty of it."

"Yes, yes," said all the officers. But not one of them saw a thing.

"Will your Majesty please undress and try on your new clothes?" asked one cheat. "Then you can see in the mirror how splendid you look."

The emperor took off his clothes and they pretended to put on him each part of the new suit. They pretended they were tying something around his waist. Then they pretended to tie on a train.

The emperor turned around and around before the mirror.

"How becoming the new clothes are, your Majesty!" said the men. "They are gorgeous robes!"

"Your soldiers are waiting outside with the canopy that will be carried over you," said the parade master.

The emperor looked at himself again in the mirror. He wanted to act as if he really did like his clothes.

"They fit perfectly," he said, then announced, "I am ready!"

Two officers stooped down and made believe they were picking up the train. And up the street the emperor marched under the canopy.

"How wonderful are the emperor's new clothes!" shouted the people. "What a fine train he has to his cape!" "How his suit fits him!"

Not one of them would let it be known that he saw nothing. For if he did it would show he was not fit for his post, or that he was very stupid.

And then a little child cried out, "But the emperor has nothing on!"

"Just listen to my innocent one," said the child's father.

The crowd was silent a minute, then said, "But he has nothing on!"

The emperor felt uncomfortable, as it seemed to him they were right.

"Nevertheless, I must go on with the parade," he thought. And on he marched.

And the officers held on tighter to the train, even though there was no train at all.

THE STEADFAST TIN SOLDIER

Long ago there were twenty-five tin soldiers, all brothers, for they were made from one old spoon.

They were given to a little boy for a birthday present. When he opened the box, the little boy clapped his hands. "Soldiers, soldiers!" he shouted. He began setting them up in two rows on a table.

The tin soldiers stood tall and handsome in their red and blue uniforms. Each was exactly like the others, except one. He had only one leg. There had not been enough of the tin spoon left to finish him. But he stood as straight as his brothers. And he was the soldier who was to become famous.

The little boy placed him in front of a cardboard castle on the table. Around the castle was a lake made from a mirror. Toy swans swam on it and little trees stood nearby.

In the doorway of the castle stood a beautiful paper lady wearing a dainty white dress. A blue scarf hung over her shoulders. On it was pinned a huge, shiny rose. Her arms were lifted gracefully, for she was a dancer. She held one leg so high it was hidden under her ruffled skirt.

Because he could see only one of the little dancer's legs, the tin soldier decided she had only one leg like himself.

"She would be the very wife for me," he thought. "But she is much too grand. She lives in a castle. I have only a box with my brothers."

However, he was a steadfast tin soldier, so he did not give up easily. "I will try to get to know her," he said to himself. He lay down behind a snuff-box and watched her.

The little dancing lady kept right on standing on one leg. Not once did she rock or slip.

After the little boy went to bed that night the toys began to play. They made believe they were having a battle.

The twenty-four soldiers that had been put back in the box rattled the lid. They wanted to join the others.

The nutcrackers turned heels over head.

The pencil wrote on the slate.

There was such noise that the canary woke up and began to sing.

The only two who did not move were the tin soldier and the little dancer. She stood on tiptoe, with her arms outstretched. He stood on his one leg and watched her moment after moment.

Ding-dong! The clock struck twelve. Up popped the snuffbox lid. Out came a little goblin! He was something like a jack-in-the-box.

"Tin soldier!" said the goblin. "It is not polite to stare at the fine lady."

The tin soldier pretended that he did not hear the goblin.

112

"Oh, you just wait until tomorrow," said the goblin.

Next morning the little boy placed the tin soldier on the window sill. The window flew open.

Now, it could have been the goblin that did it. Or maybe the wind did it. However it happened, the little soldier fell headfirst down to the street.

It was a terrible fall. He landed on his head, his leg straight up and with his bayonet stuck between the paving stones.

The little boy went to look for him but he could not find him.

If the tin soldier had called out, "Here I am!" the boy would have heard him. But being a soldier, he did not think it right to ask for help.

Later, it began to rain. It rained very hard. When it stopped, two boys came by and found the tin soldier.

One of them picked him up. "We can make a boat," he said, "and let him go for a sail."

The boys made a boat out of newspaper and put the tin soldier in it. Then they put the little boat in the gutter.

The water ran swiftly. The boat rocked back and forth. Sometimes it whirled around.

The tin soldier trembled once. But he soon gained back his courage and remained steadfast.

Suddenly, the boat went under a long wooden tunnel. It became as dark as it had been in his box.

"Where am I going now?" the tin soldier wondered. "It is all the fault of that goblin! If only the little lady were with me, I would not mind anything."

The stream became stronger and the boat began to fill with water.

The water rose to the tin soldier's knee, then to his waist. Soon, it was up to his neck. As it covered his head he thought, "Will I ever see the little lady again?"

Deeper and deeper he sank. The paper gave way.

"What is happening to me?" he wondered as he felt something very strange.

The tin soldier had been swallowed by a big fish!

And, oh, how dark it was inside the fish! It was

worse than in the tunnel. But the tin soldier was brave as always. He lay full length, holding his bayonet over his shoulder.

The fish bounced and flipped about wildly. Then at last it became quiet. It did not move for a very long time.

Suddenly the tin soldier saw something like a streak of lightning pass by. He was in the daylight again.

A voice shouted, "Look what I found inside the fish!"

The fish had been caught and sold at a market. The cook had cut it open in order to bake it for dinner.

Quickly she carried the tin soldier into the sitting-room for everyone to see.

He was placed on a table. It seemed impossible, but it was true. It was the very same room he had been in before! There were the same toys. There was the same castle on the table. And in the castle doorway stood the graceful little dancer.

The tin soldier was so happy to see her he almost cried. But instead, he stood tall and brave. He looked

116

at her and she looked at him.

The little boy was very pleased to have the tin soldier back. He placed him beside the other soldiers.

Then, without warning, the boy's brother grabbed the tin soldier and threw him into the fire. It may have been the goblin that caused him to do such a terrible thing.

The tin soldier stood straight, the flames leaping around him. His bright colors disappeared. He looked at the little dancer and she looked at him. He looked at her again and she looked at him.

As they looked at each other, a door suddenly blew open. The tin soldier trembled as he saw what was happening.

The wind blew the little dancer straight into the fire beside him! The flames leaped higher. Then she was gone.

Seconds later, the tin soldier was burned into a lump. When the ashes were taken out all that was found of him was a little tin heart. Beside it lay the little dancer's once-shiny rose. It was burned as black as coal.

THE LITTLE MERMAID

Far out, the sea is as blue as cornflowers and very, very deep. Many tall buildings, one on top of the other, would not reach from the bottom to the surface. And, way down deep live the sea people.

Now, you must not believe there is nothing but sand on the ocean floor. There are many strange trees. There are plants and flowers. All kinds of fishes swim among them. And at the deepest spot

119

of all there is a wonderful sight! It is the castle of the sea king!

The walls of the castle are made of coral and the windows are of amber. But the most surprising part is the roof. It is made of mussel shells which open and close with the movement of the water. In each shell there is a gleaming pearl. Any one of the pearls would be perfect in a queen's crown.

The sea king once lived there. The sea king's wife was dead, so his mother kept house for him.

She was a wise woman and proud of her noble birth. To show that she was royal she wore twelve oyster shells on her tail. Other high-born ladies were allowed to wear only six.

The sea king's mother was also very kind. She took splendid care of her six little granddaughters.

The little sea princesses were very beautiful, but the youngest was the prettiest of all. Her cheeks were like rose petals. Her eyes were as blue as the sea. And, like the other sea people, she had no feet, only a fish's tail.

Every day the princesses played in the castle. When the amber windows were open the fishes

swam in to visit them. The fishes ate right out of the princesses' hands, and let themselves be petted.

Outside the castle there was a garden. It was too marvelous to even imagine.

Trees sparkled with golden fruit. Hundreds of flowers nodded bright blossoms. The earth was a deep blue sand. And a strange blue mist covered everything. It was as if one were up in the sky instead of down in the sea.

Each of the princesses had a small garden of

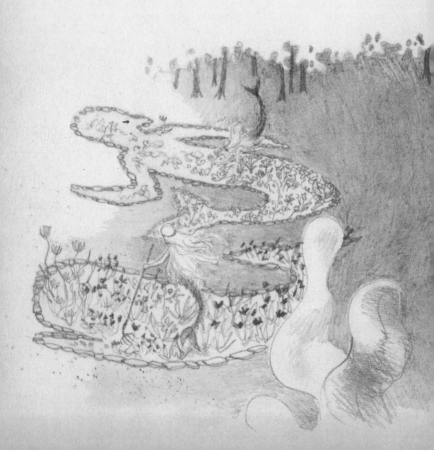

her own to plan and care for.

One princess made her flower bed in the shape of a whale.

Another sister made hers in the form of a mermaid.

But the youngest princess made her garden as round as the sun. And in it she planted only flowers as red as the sun. In the center she placed a marble statue of a boy. She had found it at the bottom of the sea where it had fallen from a ship.

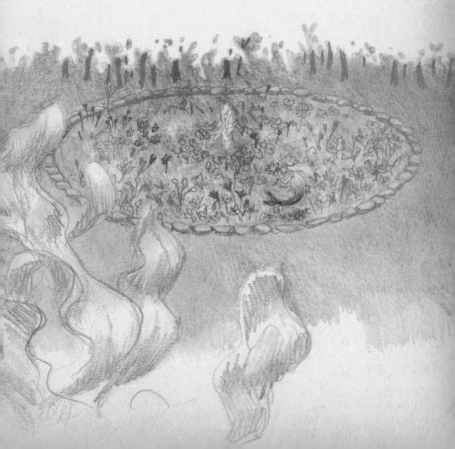

The youngest princess loved her garden. But her greatest happiness was hearing about the world up above.

Over and over she said to her grandmother, "Please tell me about the towns and people! And about the animals, too."

The grandmother always answered these questions if she could. One day she said, "The fishes sit in the trees and sing beautiful songs."

"Fishes singing!" said the little mermaid. "What surprises there are up there!"

It was the birds that the grandmother had called fishes, of course. The little mermaid would not have understood about birds, for she had never seen one.

"When you are fifteen you may go to the surface," her grandmother told her. "You can sit on the rocks and watch the ships sail by. And you can see the forests and towns."

"But, oh, what a long time! How shall I wait five years?" the little mermaid sighed. "There are so many things to know, and I am in a hurry."

The oldest sister beamed with happiness. "I go

up this year! I will tell you about everything I see," she promised.

Weeks passed and months passed. And then came the oldest princess's fifteenth birthday. There was great excitement as she got ready to go to the surface.

"Please do not stay long," begged the youngest mermaid. "I can hardly wait to hear about what is up there."

"I shall do my best," the oldest said, and swam away.

When she returned her five sisters were waiting at the castle door. "Tell us! Tell us!" they shouted.

"There are many wonderful things!" the oldest princess replied. "Best of all was seeing the lights of a town and hearing music! The lights twinkled like stars and church bells rang. I also heard people talking." She gave a deep sigh. "I wish I could have gone into the town. But I could only lie on the beach, of course."

The little mermaid was charmed by what she heard. "How glad I will be when I too can go," she said.

Many nights she stood by the window and dreamed of the great town. She even imagined she heard the bells ringing.

The next year the second sister went to the surface. She saw the world at sunset.

"It was the most beautiful sight I have ever seen," she said on her return. "The heavens looked like gold! The clouds were rosy-red and violet! I swam toward the sun, but it sank and the colors faded away."

The year after that, the third sister had her fifteenth birthday. Up and up she swam.

"I am going to be bold and go far away," this sister thought. So she went up a broad river that flowed into the ocean.

When she came back to the castle, all the princesses gathered to listen.

"I saw green hills and huge forests," she told them. "At one place by the shore, I came upon many little children."

"Oh, tell us about them!" the other sisters cried.

The third sister shook her head sadly. "I wanted to play with them, but they were afraid of me and

126

ran off. Then a little black animal came along. It barked and barked! I was frightened, so I hurried out to the open sea."

When the fourth sister returned from her adventure she said, "I stayed out in the big waters! I could see for miles and miles. The sky was like a glass dome." She clapped her hands happily. "There were dolphins turning somersaults! And giant whales spouted water like fountains!"

And then it was the fifth sister's turn. Her birthday came in winter.

"I did not see the things you did," she said when she was back in the castle. "The sea was green! Icebergs as big as mountains floated about! They were shaped in marvelous ways and sparkled like diamonds."

"Did you see any other wonderful things?" the youngest sister asked eagerly.

"Oh, yes!" said the fifth sister. "Late in the evening, thunder roared. There were streaks of lightning across the sky. And the icebergs were lifted up by the powerful waves!"

Now that the five princesses had seen what was

above the water they were no longer interested in going up again. "No place is more delightful than our home," they said.

However, they did rise sometimes. If they found a ship tossed by a storm, they sang sweetly. They were trying to tell the people on the ship not to be afraid.

Each time the sisters went to the surface, the youngest wished to go with them.

"Will my fifteenth birthday ever come?" she wondered. "I have waited and waited for it."

She would have wept if she could, but mermaids do not have tears.

At last, the longed-for day arrived!

"Now you may go to the top," said the grandmother. "Come, I will dress you like your sisters."

She gave the little mermaid a wreath of white lilies. On each petal was half a pearl.

"How beautiful!" the little mermaid said, and put the wreath on her head.

Then the grandmother fastened eight oysters to the princess's tail. By wearing them she showed her royal birth.

129

The little mermaid cried out, "O-o-o, it hurts!"

"One must suffer to be beautiful," her grand-mother told her.

The little mermaid thought, "I would much rather wear the flowers from my garden." But she did not dare to say it aloud. And anyway, she was so happy and excited, it did not really matter.

"Good-bye, good-bye!" she called gaily as she floated upward like a bubble.

The sun had just set when her head rose above the water.

The little mermaid stared with delight! The clouds were rose tinted. The evening star twinkled at her.

"It is more wonderful than I imagined!" she thought, overjoyed.

Soon she saw a ship not far away. The air was so quiet she could hear voices singing.

The little mermaid was curious. She swam right up to the cabin window. As the waves lifted her she could see the people inside. They were dressed in fine clothes and having a party.

Then the little princess gasped with surprise. Among the people was a most handsome prince!

She watched him closely, her heart fluttering.

When the sailors began dancing on the deck, the prince joined them.

The little mermaid listened and learned it was the prince's sixteenth birthday. That was the reason for the gay party.

"Oh, how very handsome he is!" she sighed.

The dancing continued and the little mermaid could not turn her eyes away.

It was quite late when the lights were put out. The ship began moving as sail after sail was opened in the wind.

Huge waves tossed the little mermaid up and down, but she was not afraid. A few more minutes, and the waves rose higher and higher. Then lightning flashed across the sky.

She saw the sailors pull down the sails. Their ship was tossed about in the angry sea.

The little mermaid smiled. "They are having a merry time," she thought.

Then she heard the ship creak and groan. Crash went the mast! The ship tipped to one side and the sea washed over it!

"I must save the prince!" the little mermaid cried.

She swam quickly between the pieces of the broken ship. She remembered the prince was not like the sea people. She thought, "What can I do? Oh, I must save him!"

She went down deep and rose high again on the waves. Again she dived. And again and again.

Finally, she found the prince! He was so tired his eyes were closing.

The little princess held his head above the water and let the mighty waves carry them. "I have saved him, I have saved him!" she thought happily.

They floated all night and by dawn the storm was over. The sun shone on the water and seemed to bring color to the prince's cheeks. But his eyes were still closed.

The little mermaid kissed his brow. "He is so like the statue in my garden," she thought. "How I do wish he might live."

Not far off was a shore lined with green forests. "I will carry him there," the little mermaid decided.

At last the prince lay on the sand. Bells rang from a white building hidden among the trees. A group of girls came running toward the beach.

The little mermaid swam away and hid behind some rocks. From there, she watched.

The girls found the prince and went for help.

After a while, the little mermaid saw the prince move. He smiled at those who stood around him.

"He does not smile at me," the little princess thought sadly. "He does not know I am here, or that it was I who saved him."

When she saw him carried into the building, she swam slowly back to the sea castle.

"What marvelous things did you see?" asked her sisters.

"A ship sunk by a terrible storm," was all the little mermaid would say.

Many, many times after that she returned to the beach where she had left the prince.

"If only I could see him again!" she said.

But never once did her wish come true. And each time she was sadder than before.

Finally, she could bear it no longer. She told one of her sisters her secret. All at once, the other sisters knew it. Soon their mermaid friends knew it, too.

"I know where the prince lives," one of the friends said. "I met him at a party in his honor."

"Come, little sister," said the princesses. "We will go through the sea to his palace."

They joined hands and floated upward as they had been told.

On the shore stood a shining palace. Marble steps led from it down to the sea shore. Through the tall windows could be seen silk curtains and fine furniture. The grandest thing of all was a fountain, its spray shooting high into the air.

Now that the little mermaid knew where the prince lived, she returned there often.

One day she found a little creek that ran underneath the palace balcony. There she could sit and watch the prince as he sailed in his fine ship.

Sometimes she floated close beside the ship, listening to the crew. When she heard them say, "The prince is a splendid young man," she was very pleased. To know he was liked by others filled her with happiness.

And more and more the little mermaid longed to be among humans. Their world seemed much

136

more wonderful than her own.

"Do humans die as we do?" she asked her grandmother.

"Yes," the old lady told her. "Their lifetime is shorter than ours. We can live to be three hundred years old. But when we die we turn to foam on the water."

The little mermaid did not understand. She frowned and asked, "What happens to humans?"

"They have a soul," the grandmother said. "After humans die, their souls live on. They rise to a beautiful unknown place we shall never see."

The little mermaid frowned again. "Why are we not given a soul so that someday we may go to that beautiful place? I would give all my three hundred years to be a human one day."

Her grandmother looked at her lovingly. "Do not worry about it," she said. "We are happier and better off this way."

But the little princess *did* think about it. Another time she asked, "Can I do nothing to become a human?"

"It could only happen if a human loved you

dearly," said the old lady. "He would have to marry you. Then you would share the happiness of human beings." She shook her head sadly. "It can never be! Your fish's tail is beautiful, but the earth people think it very ugly. They have strange things called legs."

The little mermaid gave a deep sigh. She looked with sorrow at her fish's tail.

"Come, let's make merry," her grandmother said. "Let's leap and jump, and dance and sing. We must enjoy our three hundred years!"

The little princess sang with a sweet voice. It was lovelier than any of her sisters'. When they clapped for her she was happy for a while.

But soon she began to think again of the world above. Neither did she forget the handsome prince. She slipped out into her garden. There she sat quietly and wished for a soul like his.

Suddenly, the little mermaid heard music. The sound of bugles came down through the water!

"Maybe it is the prince sailing overhead!" she thought hopefully. "I would gladly give up everything for him!"

After trying to plan a way to win him, she decided to go to the sea-witch.

"She has always frightened me," the mermaid remembered with a shudder. "But perhaps she can help me." So the little mermaid swam away in a direction she had never been before.

She struggled through whirling waters. And against a strong tide. Then she entered a strange forest. The trees and bushes were half plant and half animal. They looked like snakes, each with a hundred heads!

The little mermaid's heart pounded, and she almost turned back. But she thought of the prince and regained her courage. "I will go forward!" she said.

It took all her strength to push her way to a clearing. And there in the middle was a house built of wood from a wrecked ship. Before the door sat the old witch.

"I know what you want," said the witch. "You are very foolish, for your wish will bring nothing but trouble." She let out a mean, screeching laugh.

The little mermaid trembled. "How can anyone be so loud and ugly?" she thought.

141

The witch grinned and said, "You want to get rid of your fish's tail and walk on stumps instead!" And again she let out the awful screech. "I will mix a brew for you. You must swim to shore and drink it before the sun rises."

"I will," the mermaid said softly.

An old iron pot stood over a fire. The witch put all kinds of things in it.

While she stirred and stirred the brew, she said, "You must pay me for this. I shall have your lovely voice." She laughed again. "You think you will charm the prince with it, but you will not be able to speak!"

"Please do not take my voice," the little mermaid begged. "What shall I have left?"

"Your beautiful form and graceful movements," said the witch. "And above all, your sparkling eyes. They are enough to charm anyone."

The little mermaid put her fingers on her lips. Her heart was breaking. If she had had tears she would have cried and cried.

"Here you are," said the witch, handing her the brew. It was as clear as water.

Again the little mermaid thought of the handsome prince. Yes, she would even give up her voice for him! She took the brew and swam away.

She reached the prince's palace before the sun came up.

Without looking back at the sea, the little mermaid drank the brew. Her throat burned. Pain shot through her body. In an instant she fell as if dead.

When the sun spread its warmth over the little mermaid, she awoke. She looked up and could not believe what she saw. There, bending over her, was the prince! His coal-black eyes smiled at her kindly.

As she looked down she saw that her fish's tail was gone. Instead, she had pretty white legs!

"Who are you?" the prince asked.

The little mermaid smiled at him with her shining eyes. She tried to tell him, but she could not say a word.

The prince took her by the hand and led her to his palace.

Oh, how painful was every step the little mermaid took! Her feet felt as if she were walking on sharp glass.

"But I am with the prince," she said happily to herself.

And on she walked as lightly as a bubble, gladly bearing the pain.

At the palace she was given clothes of silk and velvet. She was the fairest of all who lived there.

That night, beautiful slave girls sang before the prince. When he clapped his hands and smiled, the little mermaid was sad. She knew her voice had been lovelier than theirs.

"If only I could sing for him!" she wished.

And then the slave girls began to dance.

The little mermaid rose on tiptoe. She lifted her arms and moved gracefully across the floor. She danced as no one had ever danced before!

Everyone was enchanted. And most of all, the prince. He clapped and smiled and clapped.

The little mermaid danced on and on. Her heart beat fast with happiness, even though her feet stung with pain.

The prince said, "You must live here at the palace."

He had more clothes made for her, and a satin

cushion for her to sleep on.

At night when the others were asleep, the little mermaid often went outdoors. She liked to put her burning feet in the cool water and to think of her home at the bottom of the sea.

One night her sisters appeared, singing sad songs. "We wish you had not left us," they told her.

Another night, the little mermaid saw her grandmother near the shore. Her father the sea king came, too. They stretched their arms toward her.

"I am sorry to be away from them," thought the little mermaid. "But I could not bear to leave my prince."

One day the prince told her, "You are more faithful to me than anyone. And you are so like a young girl who saved my life. I was on a ship that sank and she found me on the shore." He smiled tenderly and added, "She is the only one I could truly love. You are very like her."

"How sad for him," thought the little mermaid. "He does not know it was I who held him up and floated with him all night."

Not long after that, the prince said, "I am to

go away. My father says I must visit the daughter of another king. But I do not want to marry her."

He kissed the little mermaid's lips. "If I had to choose a bride, I would choose you," he said.

She was delighted when he took her on the voyage with him. Church bells rang as their ship neared the great city. From tall towers trumpeters blew horns. And on the streets soldiers stood at attention.

"This is all very wonderful!" thought the little mermaid. "And now to see the king's daughter. I hope she is not so beautiful that she will charm my beloved prince."

She had to wait until the fancy ball that night to see the princess. As she stared at the maiden's graceful form, she held her breath.

"Oh, she is very, very beautiful!" thought the little mermaid. "Her skin is like satin. Her blue eyes sparkle like the sea in the sunshine."

The little mermaid frowned with worry.

As the prince bowed to the princess, he said with joy, "It is you! You who saved me when I lay on the shore!"

He turned to the little mermaid and said, "My

wish has been granted! I know you are happy that I have found her."

The little mermaid kissed his hand, but her heart was broken.

"Is it to be as the old witch said?" she thought with fright. "Have I given up my voice, only to have sadness? Am I to become foam on the sea if my prince marries this princess?"

And it came about just as the little mermaid feared. The prince and princess were married the next day.

The little mermaid was dressed in silk and gold, and carried the bride's long train. But she heard nothing and saw nothing. Over and over she said to herself, "I have lost everything."

At dark, the wedding party went aboard the prince's ship. There was a great feast. Cannons boomed! Flags fluttered! Musicians played.

The little mermaid joined in the dancing even though she was brokenhearted. "This is the last time I shall ever see my prince!" she thought. "I shall never have a soul like his. For now I shall become foam upon the sea."

It was past midnight when the party ended. The prince and his bride went to rest in a splendid tent on the deck. All became quiet on the ship.

The little mermaid stood by the rail and looked toward the east. She dreaded the sunrise.

Just then, her sisters rose out of the water. They looked pale and sad. Their long hair did not flutter behind them.

"We gave our hair to the sea witch so that she would help you," they called out. "Here is a sword she sent you! You must strike the prince with it before the sun comes up!"

The little mermaid wanted to say, "No, no, I could never do that!" But all she could do was shake her head.

"But you must! The sea witch said it is the only way to save yourself," the sisters said. "When the prince falls at your feet, you will get back your fish's tail!"

Again the little mermaid shook her head.

"You must!" the sisters begged. "Then you can come down into the sea and live your three hundred years. Hurry! The sun is about to rise."

They sighed and disappeared.

The little mermaid tiptoed to the tent and pulled back the curtain.

The prince was sleeping beside his bride.

The little mermaid looked at him with all the love in her heart. She bent and kissed him.

The first light of dawn came through the open curtain.

The little mermaid raised the sword! But then she looked at the prince's handsome face again. Her arm trembled. Her thoughts whirled dizzily.

"No, no! I can not do it!" she said. She flung the sword into the sea. Then she threw herself into the water.

The sun shone brightly. Above the little mermaid appeared hundreds of spiritlike beings. They were beautiful! The little mermaid could see through them as if they were a veil. They had no wings and floated by their own lightness through the air.

And then a surprising thing happened. The little mermaid saw that her body was like theirs! More and more she was being freed from the foam.

"Where am I floating to?" she said aloud. Her voice had returned! It sounded sweeter than any music she had ever heard!

The spiritlike beings answered, "To the daughters of the air. We have no souls, either. But we gain souls by our good deeds."

The little mermaid raised her veil-like arms toward the sun. For the first time she felt tears in her eyes.

"We go to hot countries and bring them cool breezes," the daughters of the air told her. "We

spread the sweet smell of flowers over the world. When we have tried to do good deeds for three hundred years, we receive a soul."

The little mermaid smiled at them with wonder.

"You have suffered a broken heart, but your courage has brought you to us," said one of the daughters of the air.

Suddenly, there was a great shout from the ship.

The little mermaid saw the prince and his bride looking down in the water for her.

And now that the little mermaid was invisible, she kissed the bride. She smiled lovingly at the prince. Then she soared into the clouds with the air children.

"In three hundred years we shall find that beautiful unknown place," they told her.

One of them whispered, "We may reach it sooner. Every time we float into the home of a kind, loving child, we have a year less to serve."

"But if we find one who does not mind his parents, we will weep," said another air child. "And every tear adds another day to our time."

The little mermaid smiled contentedly.

Whitman TWEEN-AGE BOOKS

IN-BETWEEN BOOKS FOR
IN-BETWEEN READERS

**TALES FROM
HANS CHRISTIAN ANDERSEN**
as told by Katharine Carter

**TALES FROM
THE ARABIAN NIGHTS**
as told by Lee Wyndham

ADVENTURES WITH HAL
by Gladys Baker Bond

IT'S A MYSTERY!
Stories of Suspense
by Mildred Bingham

MYSTERY AT REDTOP HILL
by Marjory Schwalje

GOLDEN PRIZE
And Other Stories
About Horses

**KENNY
AND HIS ANIMAL FRIENDS**
by Joan Talmage Weiss

*Not too easy,
Not too hard,
Just LOTS OF FUN!*